UPGRADE_ 1.0

UPGRADE_1.0

ZION'S ASCENSION
ADVENTURES

N.K. WATSON

UPGRADE_1.0: ZION'S ASCENSION ADVENTURES

First published 2021

Body Temple
Publishing

Published by Body Temple Publishing,

Email: bodytemple@live.com.au

Printed by: Independently Published

UPGRADE_1.0: ZION'S ASCENSION ADVENTURES

N.K. Watson

ISBN: 978-0-6452434-9-9

Dedication –

For my son Aydan who inspires me every day.

"Yesterday I was clever, so I wanted to change the world. Today I am wise, so I am changing myself" – Rumi.

Table of Contents

Preface

Welcome, to those have joined me for the first time, I invite you to open your mind and enjoy the journey ahead. For those who have returned welcome back friend and please enjoy the adventure. I have immersed myself in the unknown and metaphysical world of energy, frequency and vibration for some time now and not much surprises me anymore. I have researched many modalities of energy healing and become a certified beyond quantum healer using hypnosis as my main connection to the higher self of others. This deeply exploratory work has led me to uncover an array of weird and wonderful remembrances for my clients. Many of their stories are included in my books. These stories have come through past life regression sessions I have guided them through. Some narratives have been embellished for theatrical and storytelling reasons.

I believe the subconscious is the key to healing anything and everything if it is warranted. Through my journey of self-discovery and the integration of the self I have come to realise that to heal physically is not the main event, it is in the journey and awareness of the true self that is the true awakening.

I felt the need to write my thoughts, and my revelations down, melded all in one place, firstly to make sense of them all and secondly to aid others in learning what I feel are universal laws and sacred knowledge hidden in plain sight.

I began by supporting my partner through his cancer scare and evolved into wanting to help the whole of humanity. Now I know that through service to others I am in turn healing parts of myself, my traumas that are reflected to me through what I see without, I am ultimately healing my within. I truly believe that through the integration of the self I can manifest what I desire to experience and begin to heal the whole of humanity. Which is merely me reflecting back to my eternal self.

I hope to inspire others to look within, to expand their minds and to realise that they are divine eternal beings of light who can with a variety of different perspectives and remembrances start to take more responsibility and direction in their own lives. To meld and create the lives they want to live not just the lives they find themselves in. I want humans to know that there is a higher purpose, and they can receive guidance if they just stop for a moment and go within and listen to the quiet voice of their higher self. This higher dimensional part of themselves which has already experienced all the layers and lessons and has evolved to a higher awareness. One who can guide them in each decision they have to make, hold space for them and support them through the difficult times. We all have so much support from the higher realms, we must begin to harness this powerful energy for ourselves and the greater good of humanity.

In Love & Light,

N.K. Watson.

Disclaimer

I have written this book in a fictional sense. Some names, characters, places, and incidences may have occurred during sessions of clients under hypnosis but have been adjusted to the clients' request. Much of the story is channelled through my own higher self and imagination. Any resemblance to actual persons, living or dead, groups, businesses, companies, events or experiences is entirely coincidental.

The information shared in this book is for personal use only and does not constitute endorsement of any website or other source. In the event you use any of the information in this book for yourself, the author and the publisher assume no responsibility for your actions.

~ Level 1 ~

Nexus

He felt stuck, he was immersed in complete darkness, all he could sense was a feeling of pressure all over his body and a tingling in his hands. His hands felt as though they were inside out or bent backwards somehow. He sat with these feelings surrounding him and took some deep breaths, after what seemed like only minutes he suddenly emerged like out of an egg into an unknown world. A world where all around him all he could see were large walls of dark purple amethyst crystals with jagged edges. The earth beneath him was covered with white glistening sand and there was no plant life for as far as his eyes could see, nothing green to contrast or soften the stark jaggedness of the razor-sharp crystal walls. He looked around trying to understand what he was doing here; he still held the feeling of his hands being backwards. As he looked down at his hands, he saw they were in fact bent at the wrists like an insect. He looked down at his feet and legs and could sense that he walked with his legs bent and crouched down like an invertebrate. With anticipation he took a look at himself in the reflection of one of the crystal walls, what he saw was a shocking sight staring back at him. He looked like a praying mantis, bogley eyes and all, he had beige skin and scurried around on his hind legs farming the planet.

He felt a strong sense of purpose, he was there on some kind of a mission. He was there to harness the healing energy of these magnificent crystals, store it within himself and his ship and transport it back to his home planet.

When he had siphoned all he could of the healing energy he took off in his ship and returned home. Flying his ship with only his thoughts, using his consciousness to steer the ship home.

His home planet was filled with praying mantis just like him, they were part of his hive. They were happy to see him return and helped him download the energy into massive quartz crystal monoliths already constructed on the planet. These monoliths were used to store the energy and slowly discharge it out into the atmosphere where the inhabitants would absorb the healing energy for their own optimal health.

Eventually over several years the collective race constructed large obelisk quartz crystal pillars with tapered tops that would electromagnetically harness the healing energy from the planet of the dark amethyst crystals. There was no need for the Mantis race to return to that planet anymore as they could harness all they needed through these monumental pillars which downloaded the energy directly to the quartz monoliths.

Zion awoke dazed and confused. What was that all about? What a crazy dream he thought to himself.

Later that day Zion and Eli sat watching YouTube together in Zions room, there were chip and chocolate packages strewn all over the floor and a distinct odour of teenage boy in the air. As Zion glanced across at his best friend of over 12 years, he knew exactly what he was thinking... Pizza.

"Hey Eli, do you feel like pizza?" he asked.

"How did you know?" replied Eli, looking at him with his wide brown eyes, which matched his dark brown hair.

People had always assumed they were brothers as they looked so similar, except for the fact that Zion had blue eyes. They were both tall for their age, strongly built and had a calm air about them. They had been friends since kindergarten where they hit it off at the fence while checking out all of the cars at the mechanic next to the school. They both loved cars, anything to do with cars, they had both memorised each and every car built from 1960 upwards. It was like they were kindred spirits destined to meet and enjoy a life together. All of the other kids didn't really understand Zion and Eli, they were all interested in childish things. Zion and Eli seemed to be old souls, more interested in grown up things and they both somehow understood what the adults talked about much better than their counterparts.

Zion Blaze wasn't just any normal kid, growing up he had always felt a little different to everyone else. He could feel what others around him were feeling, he knew their thoughts before they would say anything out loud. He felt like he was tapped into some sort of Universal field of information, picking up things like a portable Wi-Fi device. All of his life he wasn't really sure what to make of it all, to him it was his normal default.

"Let's go make a pizza" Zion instructed to Eli.

Up they got and as they both walked to the kitchen they came across Zia, Zion's twin sister in the hallway. They were identical twins but obviously being a female Zia was much prettier and got a lot of attention from the boys at school. She stayed mostly in her own world, her and Zion were close but respected each other's space as they both enjoyed being alone with their individual thoughts.

Eli did his usual embarrassed look as Zia passed them and continued following Zion to the kitchen almost tripping over his own feet. Zion knew Eli had a crush on his sister since they were in second grade but they never talked about it. It just wasn't something they talked about, not yet anyway. It was kind of awkward anyway seeing she was Zion's twin.

As they entered the kitchen Zion's mum joked "Boys, you made it out of the dungeon."

Mr. & Mrs. Blaze were pretty cool parents, they took a more relaxed approach to parenting. Their philosophy was, "what you fight you strengthen and what you resist persists" meaning even if they pushed their children to do something they knew they would resist all the more and they would never achieve their desired outcome. So, to a degree they let them learn their own lessons, sometimes the hard way but they believed that was the purpose of life, to work through life lessons and evolve to a higher awareness.

After Zion and Eli had consumed their pizza, it was time for Eli to go home, he didn't live far away and could walk the three blocks to his home where he lived with his Mum and little brother.

Zion and Eli had spent their whole weekend watching scary videos on YouTube. Everything Zion had seen was at the forefront of his mind when he went to bed that night along with the strange dream he had encountered the night before. It was hard for him to fall asleep as every sound and any motion made him remember the spooky things he had seen on the videos earlier in the day. He decided to go to the kitchen and make a fruit smoothie, they usually helped him fall asleep. He mixed fresh banana, some vanilla essence which looked as though it was from the 1970's, and some milk. He returned to his room finishing the smoothie as he walked and flopped down onto his bed ready for sleep.

Finally, he fell asleep and started to dream a dream where he seemed to be drifting and floating, floating and drifting, flying through the sky wrapped up in a soft fluffy cloud. As he drifted, he saw fractals of light waves fly past him as though the alternate universe he found himself in was having a battle, shooting stars and lights all around the dark black atmosphere. He strained to see out into the darkness but all he could see were more shooting lights, of all the colours of the rainbow.

Suddenly he saw a figure standing ten feet away from him; it was radiating a type of golden white light from every point of its body. It seemed illuminated from within and had a transparency where you could see the colours of the rainbow dancing within it and frequently shooting out from its body. The figure seemed to be wearing a long robe but it was connected, everything was connected with the energy of the light.

Zion's cloud floated down to the dark surface and he jumped off as the cloud dematerialized in front of his eyes. Zion did not feel threatened by this man, he felt compelled to talk to him and find out what he was doing in this strange dream. He wondered if this was a figment of his imagination reflecting what he had seen in the YouTube videos into the dream world. The bright luminescent man was gazing out in the vast distance of space in deep contemplation. Zion could not see his facial features, his face seemed blurred by so much white light radiating from it.

Zion called out, "hello", and the bright man turned to face Zion with one fluid motion and the immediate unimaginable energy he felt overwhelmed him to the point that he had to take a deep breath and collect himself before he could do anything else.

Zion could feel a powerful energy emanating from this man, it was unlike anything he had experienced before. Usually, he felt other people's emotions and energy but it was never this strong, this deeply palpable. His chest felt like it was alive and buzzing with fireflies, in fact his whole body felt like it was vibrating at such a high frequency that he could hardly contain it.

"What's happening?" he cried out to the man in obvious distress.

The glowing man stepped back and seemed to turn down his illumination, just like dimming a light globe. Zion started to see the features of the man's face, he looked kind and gentle and Zion's body started to slow down and he was feeling less shaken up.

"Please forgive me, my name is Nexus, I am a light being and have come to visit you from the planet Omega Centauri, 150 light years away from your planet Earth. I am here to give you important information to aid you in your evolution. You, my boy, are a wanderer."

Zion's mind was spinning, this was just a dream, but a cool dream at that, he might as well just go along with it he thought, see where it leads.

"Hi, my name is Zion" he replied.

"I know young man; I have been with you your whole life." Nexus said with a smile on his face, like he knew everything about him.

"What do you mean, with me my whole life?" Zion questioned.

The illuminated man continued. "I am one of your guides, an energy being of light who resides in a different dimension. I

7

evolved from your third density plane many billions of years ago and eventually moved on to the sixth density where everything is pure energy. I keep an eye on everything happening in your life and make sure you are safe to do your work. You are part of our collective complex, a group of sorts, and you volunteered to reincarnate on Earth at this extremely important time of the shift. You were sent to Earth to bring your light to Mother Earth and her inhabitants, to infuse it into the soil and the stars. You my boy possess a power within you that you have only dreamed of."

Zion's mind was blown even more than before, what was going on here, he knew this was a dream but even so it was out of this world, yet it literally felt so real. Surely it was all a dream and he would wake up soon in his bed, in his bedroom where reality would hit and shrink him back to normal. Until then he would continue the charade and see what came next.

"What is a wanderer?" Zion asked.

"Ah, yes." Nexus said with a serious demeanour. "A wanderer is a being from a different density that volunteers to help a lower density planet evolve in a much more efficient manner. Your spirit had evolved into a sixth density light being and become part of a collective complex or group as you would call it, where a merging of consciousness takes place and all is known and executed as a group. A call came out from the Confederation throughout the Universe that aid was needed on Earth. It had begun to succumb to the negative forces upon its soil, this cannot happen, so we had to step in. Although the planet Earth has a "Free Will" clause we as sixth density light beings are able to inject our spirits through various ways to be of aid to this planet.

You my boy decided to do just that. You planned a life where you had just the right parents who would give you enough freedom to evolve and remember who you truly are and why you are here. You set up the catalysts in your life to evolve to this exact moment, to bring you to the awareness you have now within this dream, which is not really a dream, I hope you understand."

Zion pondered all that Nexus had just said but his mind was seriously shattering and all he could do was nod in bewilderment.

Nexus continued. "We need you to upgrade your frequency Zion, all of the cells in your body are light manifest as matter, that light vibrates at a certain frequency range. The higher the frequency the brighter the light you can emanate onto the earth and the more powerful you become. You will then be able to receive the downloads we need to install to you to continue your very important work on Earth."

"How do I do that?" Zion asked, flabbergasted.

Nexus started to explain. "Go to the forest near your house, the one you like to visit from time to time. There is a tree growing in that forest, you will know it when you see it, it will call to you and it will glow with a luminescence, just as I do. This tree is a gateway, a portal to higher dimensional light frequencies. You must sit at its roots and close your eyes and wait. The magic will happen, just wait and be."

Zion began to ask..." But then what?"

But suddenly he felt a whizzing and a swirling feeling and, in an instant, he awoke in his bed, in his bedroom, with the feeling of complete confusion and excitement cursing through his body. He was vibrating and he could almost see his aura glowing.

Was that all just a dream? It felt so real. But it couldn't be, he was obviously asleep, dreaming. He had to get up and get ready for his day, but in the forefront of his mind he couldn't stop thinking about the dream. He decided that he would go and visit the forest after school, to see if he could find the magical tree Nexus spoke of.

Then he would have proof, or so he imagined.

~ Level 2 ~

Treeadoor

The day felt like it lasted for eons, all Zion could think about was the experience he had in his dream the night before. Meeting Nexus felt surreal and unbelievable but everything he had said struck a chord within him. It was as though the things Nexus said unearthed memories that were locked away within Zion's own mind. Subconscious memories of another lifetime imprinted within his DNA were being awoken with the remembering of such tales of different dimensions. Zion wasn't sure if this was all real or just his active imagination so he didn't dare tell anyone about it. He didn't even tell Eli, his best friend, just in case he couldn't find the magical tree and then looked like a total nut bag. He couldn't focus at all in class, there were images of the dream world flying through his mind's eye.

Finally, the bell rang marking the end of the day and Zion shot out of the classroom and ran all the way to the forest where he hoped he would find the luminescent tree. He had always entered the forest from the east side where a large hill of boulders that grouped together formed a cave. When he was younger, he used to hang out inside the cave and pretend he was hiding from native American Indians with bow and arrows. As he passed the cave a flash of what he used to imagine passed through his mind, a tall man dressed in traditional Native American Indian clothing stalked him, crouched down ready to release his arrow.

Zion pushed on, clearing the image from his mind and remembering his mission, the purpose of why he was here now. The magical tree that would upgrade his frequency, Nexus had suggested it would call to him, but how he thought could a tree call?

He wandered around the forest looking intently at each tree he came across, none of them were glowing, and none of them were calling to him. This seemed impossible, his hope waned after searching for a long while. He sat down on one of the fallen trees, he felt he was in the centre of the enormous forest. Nothing but green trees, ferns, sticks and pinecones surrounded him and possibly some birds observing his failed attempts. He sat for a while gazing out into the distance ahead, then he saw a flicker and spark reflecting directly at him. He paused and stood up, what was that, maybe someone or something was just reflecting in the sunlight. Then he heard it, it was a deep thumping sound, it felt as though the earth had a heartbeat. He started to follow the sound, he could feel the beat below his feet, it resonated into his body, coursed through his veins. It radiated into his own heart and synced together like it was becoming a part of him, or maybe he was becoming a part of it. Step by step he grew closer to the beat, then he began to see the magnificence of the radiant tree that stood disguised behind other neighbouring trees.

Finally he stood at its roots, its enormity was overwhelming, the beauty of it was majestic. He could see its glow, its purity and its power, he could sense its unconditional love, it radiated out like soft sparks of emotion toward him. He felt it all, it was just like when he saw Nexus, the striking feeling he felt of overpowering intense energy. But this time he knew why, this tree possessed extremely high energy frequencies, it was a portal to other dimensions, it was unequivocally magical.

Zion stood in awe, taking it all in, breathing the amplified energy within his soul, capturing the phenomenal sight he saw in front of him. The roots reached out far and wide above and deeply below the surface. The trunk was as thick as the width of a dodge challenger and as tall as a three-storey building. Its branches were thick and strong and inhabited the space of a large home. The leaves were green with a hint of blue and a crisping edge of golden amber, preparing to fall to the surface of the canopy floor. The entire magnificent magical tree was obviously alive with vital force energy. It swayed and moved in synchronicity with its close inhabitants like they were one. The beat of its soul was even louder than before and the distinct sound of liquid was heard pumping up and down through the roots of the tree, through the trunk and coursed upwards to the very top of this angelic beast. Hanging from it branches Zion could see glistening orbs of light, each one like a drop of water hanging downwards like a heavy glass crystal ball. As Zion focussed in on the orbs he could just make out images within the crystal sphere, they were moving as though there was a scene of a movie playing in each one.

All Zion could do was stare, he had never seen such a magnificent thing, only in dreams were such sights a reality. Then he remembered what Nexus had said to do, he had told him to sit at the tree's roots, close his eyes and just be.

Zion approached the tree, shifting closer and closer slowly. With each step he felt an energy shift take place, he integrated it and then was able to take another step forward. When he reached the trunk of the tree, he reached out and placed both his hands cautiously upon it. Immediately he felt a shock, but he didn't pull back, he stood strong. His heart began pumping faster and faster. He could then hear the heartbeat of the tree, pumping faster and faster to match his pulse. He pulled his hands away, spun around and sat at the base of the tree with his back resting up against the trunk, he closed his eyes and waited. His breath started to normalise, his mind began to clear and then a flash of brilliant white light overtook his mind's eye and all he could see was brilliant white.

After a few moments of dizzying confusion Zion once again found himself on the dark platform under the thick night sky, surrounded by whirling shooting lights. As his eyes cleared he began to become accustomed to the darkness, he again stood in awe at the sight surrounding him.

"Hello Zion." An authoritative voice boomed from behind him.

He whirled around and saw Nexus standing behind him, glowing with luminescent magnificence just as he had the previous night in his dream. His face showed an emotion of contentment that told Zion he was happy to finally see him. To be able to connect with him on a more conscious level instead of hijacking his dream states.

"Hello Nexus," Zion said. "What is happening?"

What Zion really wondered was, what the heck was going on. I mean, he enjoyed all the theatrics but what was the purpose of all of this. *What was he meant to be doing here?*, he thought as Nexus stayed quiet as though listening to his thoughts.

"Young man, I know you have many questions," said Nexus. "I will answer them all in time, but for now I need to show you your first mission."

Mission, Zion wondered, what was this, some sort of game?

"In some ways you could look at it like that my boy, but it is of high importance to the continued evolution of planet earth. Through each mission you complete you will level up and raise your frequency and likewise the frequency of those around you. You will be making changes to the lives of the characters in your life by changing circumstances for their growth and evolvement. By doing this the vibration of the surrounding earth you acquire will be raised and mother earth will be healing". Nexus explained like it was just a normal conversation.

"Ok," Zion agreed with caution, "How do I do it?"

"Do you remember that fruit smoothie you made the other night before you went to bed?" Nexus asked.

"Yes" replied Zion.

"Do you recall the vanilla essence you put in it," Nexus continued. "The one you thought looked as though it was out of the 70's?

"Yes" Zion replied.

"Well, I put that bottle of vanilla essence in your pantry, specifically for you to have" stated Nexus. "It is the nectar of the magical tree we call Treeadoor, he is an ancient Moreton Bay Fig which bears fruit. The fruit holds medicinal qualities along with psychedelic properties that aid in opening portals to other dimensions. When you consume it and go into the dream brain state you are then able to change reality with your thoughts. You can focus on something or someone and merge with their consciousness, you can send them thoughts through your mind. You are able to influence them so that they can best aid in helping humanity and the planet earth".

"We need all the help we can get at this point; the negative entities have pierced through the veil of the energetic protective quarantine. They are wreaking havoc on the susceptible minds of the humans polarised to a more negative frequency. You, my boy, need to raise the earth frequencies in favour of the positive so we can tip the scales so to speak and evolve to the new earth".

"Ok, so what do I need to do?" Zion asked, blown away by all of this information which was not making any sense to him.

"You must take the vanilla essence just before you go to bed at night. When you go to sleep the portal will open and you will be able to choose your focus for the night. You will pick a person or thing to positively influence and you will continue from there on your mission. Trust me you've got this." Nexus said with wide eyes and a big smile.

Before Zion could ask anything else Nexus was gone and he was sucked back down into his physical body sitting at the roots of Treeadoor. His mind was reeling from the expectation of changing his, and others', reality and the possibility of saving the world. Moving to the new earth, he had never heard of such a thing. *"Wasn't there only one earth?"* he thought to himself. *What was going to happen? Were they all going to be picked up and transported to a completely new planet? Would it be the same, or would it be completely different?* Zion sat for a while contemplating all these weird and wonderful thoughts. He was excited, ready for his first mission, his first journey into a new world.

That night after everyone was occupied in their rooms, Zion carefully constructed his fruit smoothie, making sure to add the same amount of the special vanilla essence he had the night this all began. He decided to hide the bottle where no one would find it as he didn't want anyone else to know his secret. This was his secret for now, his own magical world. He would share it once he understood it all much better.

He walked to his room, all ready to drink his magical potion, he got in bed and started to gulp it down. His head hit the pillow and he was out.

~ Level 3 ~

Custos & The Spiritual Library

His eyes opened and before him stood the façade of a magnificent sculptural cathedral. It seemed to be made of dark magnetic grey crystal and had a large clear crystal domed roof, resembling an enormous gazebo. Colours were refracting from the crystal and casting rainbows all around him. The large wooden door before him had a sign above it which read "Spiritualis Bibliotheca". The door began to slowly open and a glowing figure stood ushering Zion in. The figure did not talk and Zion cautiously stepped through the door following it's lead, he was not prepared for what he now saw.

There he stood in awe at the grand image presented in front of him. The entrance opened up to a gigantic sphere-shaped gallery consisting of ancient books and relics covering the entirety of the walls. Beyond was an endlessly wide corridor with numerous doors leading off to each side. Within the corridor he could see glowing figures energetically going about their business. As Zion walked forward, he could see a white marble staircase leading downwards. He edged towards the stairs and peered down. The stairs spiralled downwards and downwards as far as his eyes could see, all Zion could see was darkness many miles below the earth. This place was magnificent, it seemed to be expansive in size and energy. As soon as he had walked through the doorway his energy had heightened and he was feeling magical.

The light being beside him interrupted his thoughts and motioned for Zion to follow him; they began to walk down the spiral staircase. After a few floors he stopped at a decorative wooden door. This door was labelled "Experientia," Zion wondered what that meant and before he could speak the words out loud the usher started to speak.

"My name is Custos which is the latin name for guardian, I am here to guide you in navigating your way in this building and beyond."

"What is this place?" Zion asked.

"This is the Spiritualis Bibliotheca, or as you would call it the Spiritual Library. This building contains within its walls a compendium of all universal events, thoughts, words, emotions and intent ever to have occurred in the past, present, or future, in terms of all entities and life forms, not just human." Custos stated matter of factly.

Zion stood shocked for a moment, he was taking it all in, absorbing the enormity of what Custos had just said. This place knew everything. *"Wow, what was he meant to do here? Why was he here?"* he wondered.

Custos started speaking as though he could read Zions thoughts "You, Zion, are here to use the Experientia room. It is a place where you can choose any experience you wish. You then drop in to that experience and become at one with it. You are able to manipulate energy, manifest and create in the experience and once you are done you can come back out. What ever you do in the experience can and will change reality as you know it. So you must be careful and stick to your mission. I am here to guide you on your journey, I will be with you always, all you need to do is ask."

"How do I know what experience to choose? Zion asked.

"You will know, you will sense it and it will be illuminated just like Treeadoor and Nexus were when you saw them" said Custos.

"What is my mission?" asked Zion excitedly.

Custos started to describe in more detail. "As Nexus explained when you first met him, there is a group of negatively orientated entities called the group of Orion. They are not from this planet, they have taken up residency just outside the quarantine veil of Earth. The group of Orion entities corrupt and manipulate vulnerable humans by infiltrating negative thoughts directly into their minds. They place thoughts in the minds of these humans and use them like puppets to permeate negative energy onto Earth and corrupt society. The humans they use are, to a certain degree, vulnerable to fear distortions and are easy prey for the enslavement from the Orion entities. Your misssion is to drop into their consciousness, find their fear distortion, clear the negative energy and reset them back to their previous positive baseline by uploading an upgrade. In doing so you will be upgraded to the next level of your evolution and be able to bring more light to the world.

Zion stood, feeling shocked. What made him capable of undertaking this outlandish mission, how would he know what to do? Fear began to creep into his mind and he began to feel weak.

"You cannot let fear take over Zion, it will lower your energy field and let the negative entities tap into your mind. The level of the problem is never the level of the solution. You have been training for this mission your whole eternal life, you just don't remember. The forgetting spell is strong when you come into this realm, when you are born into the planet Earth. It must be this way so you have to work at becoming stronger, learn your lessons and then start to remember your mission. You have trained for this mission in your dream state your entire life and you have achieved this mission on other planets countless times. All you need to do is tap into the rememberance of these times. We can help you do this by downloading the programs of your previous lives lived when you accomplished these feats. Please lay down in the chair and we can begin".

Zion glanced over to where Custos was pointing and there sat a large white leather medical chair. It looked a bit like a dentist chair but much more futuristic and technical. Custos called it the 'MedBed' and he explained how it could be used for many different applications including portal journeying, information imprinting and many forms of healing.

Zion cautiously slipped into the chair and lay back. It felt extremely comfortable, the sides held his body perfectly and he almost felt like he became one with it.

Custos walked over and pressed some buttons on the display attached to the chair. Immediately a sphere-shaped orb appeared as a hologram in front of his eyes. Custos explained that each sphere of influence contained information from a different experience and time. By sending specific light frequencies through the hologram of information it would be imprinted into Zion's DNA. He would then have access to the information like it was his own regardless of whether it was or not. It was like a software upgrade to his system, like uploading a new program.

The chair began to recline backwards, the lights dimmed and the sphere of influence in front of Zion lit up. A deep sound began to reverberate throughout the room which started to make Zion sleepy. It was all so comfortable, he closed his eyes for a moment. Flashing lights began to dance around in his minds eye, geometric shapes began to form then fade then flash across from side to side. The lights began to spin and even when Zion tried to open his eyes he couldn't. He felt like he was in some kind of a trance. He made the decision to just let go, to let it all be and his whole body relaxed into the chair.

Images of other worldly scenes buzzed through his mind, strange environments, and even stranger alien beings and then suddenly he was awake. The lights were slowly dimming and the chair began to straighten up.

Zion opened his eyes, "Wow, that was insane" he exclaimed, shocked with what had just happened.

"Yes, young man, you have now been downloaded with the imprints of your relevant life memories to be successful in your mission at this time. In time you will continue to have remembrances of alternate time-lines for your continued evolution" Custos said, accomplished.

"How do you feel, do you remember?" asked Custos with a funny smirk on his face.

Zion thought for a moment. Images began to form in his minds eye, he felt he knew more, he felt he had experienced more than he had in his normal life as a 16 year old kid. He felt he had the knowledge of a 80 year old man or older, it was super weird but cool. He knew he had had experiences on other planets, this body was only on loan for now, he was experiencing so much more than what he thought he was only hours earlier. He now knew he was existing in other dimensions, in other universes simultaneously. It was all starting to make sense now, he felt ready for his first mission. He wanted to start on this journey, he had wasted enough time. It was go time.

He looked up at Custos "Yes, I remember my friend, I remember". Zion stated.

Custos looked at him still with the smirk still on his face. Zion remembered him now, they had been friends for eons.

"Now Zion," said Custos, "you must always protect yourself, especially when you enter through a portal and perform your missions. You must visualise a pyramid composed entirely of white light, it glows, it sparkles and it shimmers. I want you to mentally step into that white light pyramid, so it completely encapsulates you. This is your protection, the white light is a very powerful force and it protects against anything and everything. This powerful pyramid will stay around you protecting you for the entirety of your journey. Nothing can harm you mentally or physically. Can you see it Zion?" Asked Custos.

"Yes, I am protected" stated Zion with confidence after mentally visualising the white light pyramid surrounding himself.

"Ok, let's do this. We will start with a straight forward mission first, to get you initiated" said Custos.

Zion lay down on the leather chair again feeling powerful and focussed, what ever was going to happen he knew he was ready. Custos pressed some buttons and off he went spinning into the spherical holographic projection in front of him.

Moments later he began to see the illumination of a young boy about 16 years old alone in his bedroom. Zion flew down in his etheric body towards the boy to get a closer look at what was happening. Next to the boy lay a duffle bag filled with guns and ammunition. As the boy sat on the edge of the bed Zion could feel the boys anger and fury welling up like a fire inside of his chest. He began to feel the boys emotions and then he could hear his thoughts.

"They wont know what's coming, this will show them, they should have been my friend when they had the chance, now it's too late" said the boy in his mind.

Zion could now sense what was happening. This young man had been bullied at school, he wanted revenge and he was planning on taking these guns to school the next day. Zion had to stop this from happening, he had to find the boys fear and reveal it to the light to set him free. Zion looked around and saw a picture pinned to the boys cork board. It glowed with the same light he had seen when he first saw the glimmer of Treeadoor. The picture showed a man holding a baby, smiling with pride and joy and the caption below it read *'Bobby and Dad'*. This must be a picture of the boy as a baby being held by his father.

Suddenly Zion was sucked into complete darkness, with the overwhelming feeling of being alone and afraid. He couldn't move, all he could do was watch. Before him, projected in the darkness was a play by play of what Bobby had gone through in his life up until now. How he felt when he found out his Dad had left him when he was only 3 months old. The ongoing pain he felt from being abandoned and the fear of not being enough. Once Zion had a deep understanding of Bobby's life the screen went black for a moment and then another image appeared. This projection showed Bobby's father being enlisted into the war, he didn't want to leave his baby boy and his wife but it was his time to serve his country. He left, and then within five months he was killed and never returned.

Once the projection stopped Zion was cast into darkness once again, feeling alone and devastated.

After some time, a glowing figure began to materialise in front of Zion, the figure had an overwhelming glow of red hue. Light began to fill the space where Zion stood and his energy was once again amplified to its usual frequency. The figure stood looking at Zion and without speaking aloud started to communicate mind to mind with him. It was Alfred, Bobby's father as an ascended master and he was there to help Zion dissolve the shadow within his son. Alfred explained how he never wanted to leave Bobby and he had tried to stay with him etherically, but the shadows had gridlocked him from entering his sons field. The pain that Bobby had felt, even on a subconscious level, when his father never returned had left him vulnerable to the shadow entities. They had taken a hold over him early and were now reaping their rewards.

Bobby's father and Zion extended and focused their powerful light energy on Bobby, sending it to him and infusing it to his core. Zion sent Bobby dreams of the truth of why his father had to leave. The truth that Bobby had never been told, as his mother had been in unbearable pain and had told Bobby that his father had left them for another woman. She could not face up to the truth that he was gone forever and would never be returning.

Zion needed to uproot the initial cause of Bobby's fear which was abandonment. This was why when the other kids at school abandoned him and wouldn't be his friends he would get so angry. It was pulling on, and triggering the ingrained deep rooted fear of abandonment, the experience that had began the formation of the shadow within.

Zion and Alfred continued sending vivid dreams to Bobby of how his father had died at war and was never far away from him in spirit. Of how his Dad was always there wanting to help but because of the negative entities casting so much fear and doubt he was unable to penetrate the gridlock of the shadow.

Eventually, Zion was able to guide Bobby's etheric body away from his physical body to come and learn how to protect himself from the negative Orion entities.

Bobby joined Zion and his father in an alternate dimension where the light penetrated everything. He learned to send light and love to the negative entities as this too, was what they lacked. By sending love to them Bobby was able to loosen their grip on him and break free of their manipulation and control. It also raised their frequency towards the distortion of positivity and away from the negative. Through feeding less into the shadow of fear Bobby became stronger against the grips of the negative Orion entities.

Zion utilised his superpower of harnessing golden white light and downloaded new information into Bobby through the spherical influences containing holographic programs Custos could mobilise for him from the Spiritual Library. Zion upgraded Bobby to a higher level of awareness where he could overpower the shadow by his conscious awareness.

It took them the whole night to clear the negative, dark energy from Bobby's field, but by morning, he awoke a different young man. He awoke with a lightness he had never felt before. Instead of a mist of darkness weighing him down, he now felt the rays of the sun energising him and the colours of the world around him were magnified. He felt alive like he had never felt before, there was no fog anymore, he felt magnificent.

That day Bobby didn't take the bag full of guns to school.

That day Bobby had awoken to his true self.

That day he remembered he was loved.

~ Level 4 ~

The Universal Field

Zion awoke with a feeling of complete satisfaction. Being of service to others was liberating, he had forgotten how good it made him feel. He wondered what amazing experience he would have tonight after he gulped down his special smoothie.

He jumped out of bed and began to get ready for his day. He passed his sister Zia in the hallway on her way to the bathroom. She looked tired and confused.

"Hey Zion" she called.

Zion turned to face her.

Zia continued "Have you ever had a dream that felt so real that you wondered if it really was?" she asked with total confusion still on her face.

Zion stood for a moment, unsure how to react, or what to say. He had always had these experiences, but only over the past few nights, realised that what he had experienced in his dream state was actually real. He decided to play it down.

"Yeah sometimes, why what did you dream?" asked Zion.

Zia began to describe her dream, "I was in this place surrounded by darkness but then flashes of light began to spin around me. As I searched the area I came across a glowing man in a long white robe. He spoke to me, he said his name was Nexus and he had been waiting for me. I started to feel dizzy and then I woke up. I know it sounds crazy but it seemed so real".

Suddenly, a voice startled them, "Hurry up guys or you'll be late!" their Mum called from the kitchen.

Zia and Zion looked at each other with a look that meant 'we will talk about this later' and continued on getting ready for school.

Later that day, as Zion sat with Eli in Science class, he wondered what was happening with Zia and Nexus. Did Zia have the same powers as him, should he tell her what had been happening. He was totally unsure what to do, he had enough to think about with his own missions let alone another persons.

Mr. John loudly woke Zion from his day dream, loudly telling the whole class their new topic was going to be climate change and clean energy. Continuing on to quote the famous inventor Nikola Tesla whom invented the modern alternating current electricity supply system known as AC to us. Nikola was quoted saying "If you want to find the secrets of the Universe, think in terms of energy, frequency and vibration."

Zion thought for a moment. The secrets of the Universe; he had never even thought about the concept. How did it all work? Where did it all come from? He now knew from his dream state experiences that his energy was influenced by various people and objects. Custos also explained that he must keep his energy high to avoid dropping into the distortion of the negative. Also, the energy of the white light pyramid gave protection to whom ever visualised it. This was some sci-fi stuff but when you actually think about it, most of it actually makes a lot of sense.

Zion zoned in for a moment, almost in a trance, he was trying to find the answers to these questions. Suddenly, something popped into his mind. At that very moment Mr. John asked the class if anyone could explain the differences between energy, frequency and vibration.

Zion raised his hand, which was unusual for him as he usually stayed quiet in class and flew under the radar.

"Yes Zion" asked Mr. John, suprised.

Zion took a deep breath and began to talk. Almost as though he was channelling from a different source, the words that began to come out of his mouth were not his own.

"Vibrations refer to the oscillating and vibrating movement of atoms and particles caused by energy. Because of this, all humans and objects have an energy field that has its own vibrational frequency. Frequency, which is measured in hertz (Hz) units, is the rate at which vibrations and oscillations occur. Energy is really just thought, which is what we humans call consciousness. Energy can neither be created nor destroyed, rather it transforms from one form to another. Nothing is solid and everything is energy. There is duality within everything in the universe, because there is positive and negative energy. Everything in this universe is made up of atoms which are vortices of energy, constantly spinning and vibrating, resulting in a unique energy frequency signature."

Zion continued, like he was on autopilot and the information was just flowing through him and out of his mouth. He couldn't stop it.

He continued. "Quantum physicists have a theory which originated from the double slit experiment, which observes the behaviour of subatomic particles. The experiment reveals that the act of observation in itself, influences how the particles behave. This implies that our consciousness can change our physical reality."

Everyone fell silent for a moment, Zion began to feel uncomfortable, but then Mr. John started clapping with excitement.

"Someone has been doing their homework. Well done Zion" said Mr. John.

The rest of the day continued with unusual downloads of relevant information and synchronicities that Zion wasn't accustomed to. He started thinking things out of the blue and then within moments someone would ask him the question that corresponded with the answer he was given in his head. Other moments, he would sense that something would happen and then a little later it did. It was starting to freak him out. He would have to ask Custos or Nexus about it all tonight.

As Eli and Zion walked home they spoke about the assignment they were starting on clean energy. They were going to focus on Nikola Tesla and find out all about him and where he got his information from and what his philosophy entailed.

That night, after preparing his special smoothie, Zion lay on his bed charged but emotionally exhausted from the day. It had been a very interesting one to say the least. He was excited and ready to find out what his mission was tonight. As he drifted off to sleep he felt an electric rush like he had never felt before. It was almost like a shock of electricity cursing through his veins.

Then bam, he was standing at the front of the spiritual library in all its glory. Zion walked towards the door and pushed hard and with purpose. He was back, ready for anything. Custos greeted him in the magnificent spherical entrance and ushered him down the spiral stair case once again. Through the door of the experience room and straight into the Med Bed.

"How has your day been?" Custos asked.

"Very interesting my friend. There were lots of weird things happening today. What's that all about?" asked Zion.

"Ahhhh, you were experiencing many synchronicities today weren't you? Custos replied.

"Yes, what does that mean, why was it happening?" asked Zion.

"Well, you must be aware Zion, that where your focus goes, your energy flows. Meaning that what ever you focus on the most is where your energy flows to manifest your thoughts into reality. And if you don't take the time to focus on what matters, then you're living a life of someone else's design. For example, when you were in science class and your teacher read the quote, without knowing, you tapped into the field of knowledge, the 'Universal Field' and pulled the answer into your mind. That is how you pre-empted your teachers question and answered it correctly even before he asked it. You are levelling up and beginning to aquire insight much faster than the average human. You are becoming super aware of everything happening around you and you are tapping into the field constantly." stated Custos.

"What is this field of knowledge?" asked Zion.

"It is the Universal collection of all data recorded over eons of time, just like what is held here in the Spiritual Library. It is every thought that has been had, it is every answer that has been answered, it is every experience that has been experienced. It is eternal and alive, and because you have upgraded you are able to tap into it more easily than ever before." Custos said excitedly.

"Ok, so what you're saying is, if I focus on getting a Mustang I will get a Mustang?" Zion asked in good humour.

"Well, yes, if you put conscious thought into what the Mustang will look like, how it will feel to own it and if you can feel the feeling you will experience when you sit in it and drive it you will attract the strong possibility of owning a Mustang to yourself" explained Custos.

There are eternal possibilities in this Universe, your personal experience all depends on how you use your energy to attract these possibilities into your world. It also depends on your choices along the way and if your life plan is in line with your desires. Our script is written before we are born but it has a form of multiplicity. In a sense we are able to choose which direction we would like to follow. There are infinite possibilities determined by which direction you choose. Just like when you have a lucid dream and you are able to choose what happens next, it is one and the same. As you grow and become more powerful, manifesting will become easier and quicker. You must focus on building your energy through raising your frequency" said Custos.

"How do I do that?" Asked Zion with excitement.

"There are many ways to raise your frequency Zion. You must first understand that you are an electromagnetic being and live in a field of vibratory waves, this is the universal law of quantum physics called the law of vibration. Each human has approximately 50 trillion cells contained in their body and each cell contains, on average 0.07 volts of electricity. That means that each human is vibrating and containing 3.5 trillion volts of electricity in their body" Custos explained.

"If the environment we surround ourselves with includes higher vibrational frequencies our energy will match and resinate higher. The Law of Vibration states that everything in the Universe moves, travels and vibrates in circular motions at the sub-atomic level. Everything in this Universe carries with it a vibration that is unique to itself and carries constant movement and energy with it. At the sub-atomic level everything is vibrating and high vibrating particles are attracted to other high vibrating particles while lower vibrating particles are attracted to lower vibrating particles. In addition to our physical world, this also applies to our feelings, our thoughts, our dreams and our free will. That old saying 'like attracts like' is actually referring to how our own vibrational energy, attracts or aligns with, the same or similar vibrational energy. Literally, we are what we are vibrating. We attract our tribe of fellow souls in this manner. 'Your vibe attracts your tribe'. Your friends will give you a really good snapshot of what your vibratory frequency is. In order to change anything in your life you simply need to alter your frequency and by doing so you will attract a new vibration."

"Thankfully we have complete control over the energy we put out to the universe and therefore control over what energy aligns with ours and comes back to us. This awareness, once harnessed and understood, is incredibly powerful as you move through your life here on earth. The power of the mind is a powerful tool Zion, but only through consciously knowing what your thoughts are do you know what you are creating. The subconscious mind is like the video recorder of your mind, it has recorded all your life events from when you were in the womb through to your early years where you were in a hypnotic state of consciousness. When your mind was drawing in as much information it could, so you know now how to function in everyday life, in your community and society. The subconscious mind keeps recording each and every event in your life, positive and negative, and it stores it and replays these emotions back to you whenever there is a trigger in your current life that correlates to that past event" finished Custos.

"Wow Custos" said Zion feeling blown away by all the high vibrational information. "Maybe we should get on with tonight's mission before it's morning. I will review this information later, thank you."

"Ok Zion, but I must make you aware that last night in your mission you were stuck on the edges of the experience, operating outside of the boundaries. That is why you didn't drop into the body of the mission and why you experienced Bobby's shadow in a holding bay. You must put your protection in place and dive deep into the experience with no fear or expectations. Let it all go," explained Custos.

Zion nodded with understanding and lay back into the comfortable white leather chair. As Custos pressed the buttons he was immediately sucked into a vortex of spinning blue hues. Around and around, he whirled until he emerged onto a stark planet of dark midnight blue jagged rocks. All around him were glacial lakes of frozen water, and he could see water falls of glistening blue and soft white, clear water in the distance. He crept behind a wall of cold blue rock for protection, unsure of what to expect and continued observing the scene in front of him. This place was definitely not on Earth, it was not something he had ever seen before, at least in this lifetime. A remembrance began to emerge, and Zion began to realise that he felt a connection to this planet. He had been here before. He looked down at himself, big blue hands with only four slender fingers seemed to be attached to him. As he began to look further, he saw long blue muscular legs with skin which was almost amphibian like. Then large, webbed feet again with four toes stood below him where he stood.

What was going on?

~ Level 5 ~

Fior & The Blue Planet

After momentarily freaking out Zion realised, he had dropped into an alien body on a different planet. He had a tall, slender, blue body with a large head and big, dark, midnight blue eyes. His fingers were slim and long, and in the same formation as his toes there was only four on each appendage.

The planet Zion found himself on was the blue planet of Alsfori. A race of highly developed beings, with the same features that Zion now found himself with, inhabited Alsfori. These beings were totally self-sustaining and gentle creatures. The blue planet of Alsfori is the planet of all knowledge as the blue crystals, which make up the majority of the surface, connect and harness all universal knowledge.

Zion was an engineer who worked with the water resources of the planet in all its forms, as a gas, a liquid and as a solid. He worked along with other engineers; one of whom he could now see walking towards him. He looked similar to what Zion thought his form was reflecting at this moment in time and space.

The blue being began to talk through thought to Zion, and telepathically, he suggested they teleport to their lab. Zion agreed and within a split second they were standing in a stark white sterile room. The floor looked like stainless steel and the walls appeared to be made from a white stone of some sort. Zion's partner held a small spheroid which he placed in front of him on the floor and instantaneously a holographic matrix reflected above it. It was like a movie screen, but three dimensional, and Zion could see everything that he had been doing on this planet in the hologram. It started relaying to him points of reference of what they did on this planet so Zion could remember.

On this planet all the different states of water were used to create energy, as they fluctuated from one form to another. The highly evolved beings that occupied this planet knew that all creation was comprised of the smallest particle in the universe known as the Nimeo. The Nimeo is the nucleus of the crystal whereby the base of a crystal is light. The crystal is comprised of an extremely fine interlocking weave which forms geometric shapes. Once the crystal connects with the consciousness of the creator it mixes with other elements and through intention first creates a gaseous state, it then transforms into a liquid-water crystal and lastly into a denser solid state which can become solid matter. The crystals are manifested through the creator's consciousness through intention and necessity.

His engineer counterpart explained. "Through fusing and combining electromagnetism, sound, frequency, vibration and water we are able to create hydro-electric power. It works harmoniously, interconnectedly and interdependently with the planet and is what makes the stars and all life possible in the first place. By using currents of water energy, we are able to change the formation of the water and use it for building, electricity, and powering our ships. Through trade, we travel to different planets and galaxies to farm nutrients for our nourishment as we do not possess enough on our own planet. We use the water technology to farm the nutrients for our nourishment. We are valued by our community for our knowledge and our ways with the water. We teach our technology to each individual on our planet so that we can all work together collectively. We are the way showers and aim to show people what is possible. We would like to share this knowledge throughout the galaxies. We would like you, Zion to aid in the channelling of this information to Earth to help Mother Earth heal and give an alternative energy source to the detrimental ways you have now."

Zion's partner continued, "You must be aware of the negatively orientated beings on Earth getting their hands on this information and using it for their own benefit in a negative way. The frequency of this information is extremely high and must be kept that way. If the vibration reduces in frequency the more negatively orientated beings will be able to tap into the information and possibly use it for evil. If it stays at its high vibrational frequency, they will be unable to tap into it as it resonates too fast and it will be invisible to them."

"It must only be channelled to the human you call Mr. John; he is a scientist and engineer and will understand the importance and significance of this unprecedented knowledge. He must not disclose how he received the information as many in your history have been hurt or killed for disclosing the truth of extra-terrestrial beings passing on knowledge. One such being you learned of today, Nikola Tesla, gained much of his knowledge from higher beings not of the planet Earth. Once the government decided Tesla knew too much he was disposed of, along with all of his study and inventions" stated the blue being.

Zion stood in awe, unsure of how to speak telepathically, that wasn't explained in his download.

The magnificent blue creature explained, "It's ok Zion I can understand you; you don't need to try and speak telepathically; it will just happen automatically. You can call me Fior.

We are all multidimensional beings, so you, as this blue being in front of me, channels through to you, as Zion on Earth. Personally, I am Mr. John, your science teacher manifest, and living a parallel life here on this blue planet. We all function simultaneously on different planets and bring different aspects to each experience. Many of our high vibrational blue beings are incarnate on Earth in a human body to harness these narrow beams of frequency into the Earth. It is called the hybridisation program. Our race can only live for around 700-900 years and do not reincarnate. We hybridised ourselves so we could continue on in human physical avatars. Spending time in the school of Earth and to become embodied into the physical is highly advantageous to our evolution. We have the seeds planted on earth. It is a finely orchestrated plan that has been unfolding for many millions of years. There is no urgency of it unfolding but it is getting closer to the grand finale, the new Earth. All is going to be revealed in a much shorter space of time than any of you would even imagine. You are going to be shocked at the chaos that will unfold. But with chaos comes order as all energy integrates back into infinite harmony once again.

You as humans must stand strong in your power, you must open your heart, do not let fear overcome your thoughts. You must make the time to sit, breath and be still. You must have the courage to sit in your discomfort and see how enriching that can be. Integrating your whole being. Speaking your truth as uncomfortable as that can be at times.

If you need to make our connection stronger and tap into our field, first connect into your heart space then all you need to do it use water in different ways. Swim in it, bathe in it, stand in the rain, drink it, we communicate through water" said Fior.

Zion thought back to the first time he sensed Treeador, that thumping heartbeat reverberating through him. Everyone and everything kept telling him to tap into his heart space. It must have a relevance that Zion did not quite understand yet. It must be important.

"Yes Zion, it is of high importance, it is virtually the key to everything, it is omnipresent. Love is the highest vibrational frequency in the whole of the universe. Nothing else is higher. When you focus in on that emotion, you are connected to the universe, you become the universe. The best way for humans to connect with this power is through the heart space where the love emotion is felt. For you, you can visualise the way you felt when you connected with Treeadoor, that was when you truly tapped into your heart space. Feel that feeling and experience that emotion and you will co-create that potent connection you had with Treeadoor and you will raise your frequency beyond belief" explained Fior.

"Now that you have connected with us, the pathway for us to channel through the one you call Mr. John is clearer and more refined. He is now more lucidly connected with his sixth density Higher Self and will be able to hear the subtle communication that comes from it. We will be able to scan the planet for his unique frequency range and initiate contact. We will send light through to him more easily now and he will wonder where all this amazing information is coming from. It is now time for you to go" said Fior, motioning over to a transparent pod type structure.

"What is that?" asked Zion.

"It is your ship, a pod specifically designed by you to travel interdimensionally. All you need to do is sit in it and think of where you want to go. It taps into your consciousness and knows exactly where you need to go, and it is powered by a form of water" stated Fior.

Wow' thought Zion, his alternate blue being counterpart had created this spaceship with the use of hydropower and mind control. The conception of the mechanics and physics of designing such a contraption just blew his mind. It wasn't even worth trying to rationalise it.

Zion jumped into the ship, the seat conformed immediately to his natural physical body and felt like it held him perfectly. There were transparent controls all over the front windshield of the ship which lit up with every colour imaginable. Every part of the pod was transparent so he could see everything surrounding him. He waved goodbye to Fior, closed his eyes for a moment and started thinking of home.

Within a split second he was off, whizzing through the atmosphere, flying past strange looking planets, and massive spheres of burning lava. Up ahead he saw what seemed to look like a whirling of colours and within the colour was complete darkness. Surely it wasn't what he thought...a black hole he wondered? Before he could think anything else he was sucked straight into the deep eternal black hole.

~ Level 6 ~

Reprogramming Frequency

Zion awoke, panicking, grasping for his life and yelling out for help. He was shocked to see that he had woken up in his bedroom and seemed to be in one piece. Flying into that black hole in his ship was one of the scariest things he had ever experienced and he was glad he was back in his bed safe and sound. It took him a while to calm down from the frightening shock that had taken over his entire body.

Zion slowly got out of bed and walked to the bathroom. As he looked at himself in the mirror, he had to do a double take, he looked different somehow. He gazed into his own eyes intently and could see the newly found universal knowledge he possessed within. As he began to look over the rest of his body, he could see a subtle glowing outline surrounding his head and his shoulders. The glow had a tinge of red to it and seemed to pulse along with the beat of his heart.

He jumped in the shower and got ready for his day.

At school while he was sitting having lunch, Zion looked out into the field of students and realised he could see different colours and lights surrounding most of the individuals. Some of them had a glow about them and he could see the white light flowing upwards into the clouds. Others didn't have a glow or a darkness at all, they seemed totally void of vital energy. The remaining people had a darkness surrounding them and he could see a funnel of dark mist flowing from the sky into the tops of their heads. It was almost like there was a direct link from something dark and mysterious in the sky flowing shady information into the minds of these lower vibrational people.

Zion started to wonder if this was what Nexus and Custos were talking about? Was this the Orion group manipulating people with dark shadow thoughts? Were they directly imprinting the thoughts through this black cloud? Just as quickly as he thought it a "Yes" popped into his head. It wasn't just a yeah that's probably what's happening kind of yes from his own mind it was a strong and certain "YES" like someone was speaking to him in his mind.

"Was that you Nexus?" asked Zion with his mind.

"Yes, it is me Zion" replied Nexus. "You are completely correct; this is how the Orion entities download and imprint thoughts into the vulnerable people's minds. Now that you have upgraded to a higher frequency you are able to visually see more of the light spectrum. You can now see who they are affecting and help them directly."

"How do I do that?" asked Zion.

"When you see this happening all you need to do is tap into your heart space like Fior described last night. Look at these fellow humans and connect through them to their higher self, where you know they are perfect, eternal beings. Once you do this, the golden white light will filter through you and into them bringing powerful light to their darkness. When you can see their true self, their higher self, you aid them in uncovering that part of them too. They can then break free from the shadow and harness the ultimate power of the light within. By unlocking their true identity, you are in turn reuniting a piece of yourself with Source. Once this is accomplished the negative distortions are diminished and their hold on humanity is lessened. In time it will be banished from this earth and the new earth will form and grow to become the saviour of higher frequency beings.

The way you feel about yourself and experience life is not determined by how others look and feel about you. It is totally determined by how you look at and think about them. This is what determines your identity. We are One.

It is your reaction in the moment to them which determines your life and your experience around them." Nexus described with pure passion.

"Ok, thanks Nexus I think I understand. I will do my best to raise the frequency of these people and bring them the light." said Zion.

For the rest of the day whenever Zion encountered someone with a dark shadow engulfing them, he would tap into his heart space and transmit light to them. Zion would send the light especially to their higher self, their true self that he knew was in there somewhere, even if they didn't show it outwardly. He was starting to feel exhausted by the end of the day and once he returned home, he fell on his bed and had a nap.

As he dreamt, he connected with the 'Universal Field' where all the knowledge was stored, and a fascinating concept came through the field directly downloading into his consciousness. The concept explained how to consciously visualise and re program negative thoughts into positive thoughts. Zion decided that this could be a great method of reprogramming the shadow humans into humans of light.

The concept instructed to visualise your mind as a spherical orb inside of you and every thought you have sends out a strand of energy, a light beam of sorts. Every time you think the same thought it strengthens and extends the strand. The strand extends out from your orb into your world. It attracts similar energy as it is electromagnetic. Therefore, negative thoughts of energy strands attract and pull to you negative experiences in your world. Whereas positive thought strands attract and harness positive and enlightening experiences into your world. Instead of cutting off a negative strand, freeze it in the moment and re-adjust its frequency, raise it up to be more positive. Reprogram the negative thought by consciously changing the pattern. Then the strand will fragment off in a different direction to a higher purpose.

Zion decided he would be able to tap into other people's negative strands of thought, reprogram them by visualising their higher self and this would re-adjust the frequency to a positive distortion.

He started wondering about the people he saw that had no illumination and no darkness, the void ones. He decided to ask Nexus about them.

Nexus started explaining "Ahh, the NPC's, these are holograms of non-incarnate humans who possess no soul, no vital force, they are in a sense the non-player characters. Like in the computer games you play, the bots, the characters that the computer program controls. They are projected into the Matrix to fill the scenes. You can converse with them but they have limited responses, you would not be able to have a deep conversation with them, they possess no consciousness and no substance".

"Ok." Zion thought for a moment. "so they are only there to fill in the numbers, like backdrop people in a movie. If they are holographic and look so real, does that mean that everyone and everything else I see in my reality is holographic?" asked Zion.

"Great question my boy, you are in fact correct. This reality you sense with your limited five senses is a projection that you yourself manifest. You manifest your matrix. Everything you see, seemingly outside of yourself you are actually seeing within. Each experience you have may be stimulated by external situations where light falls upon materially manifested objects. The reflection made by these objects filter into the lens of our eyes and project an inverted image on your retina. So, what you are actually sensing and perceiving is always within you. We must stop looking outside of ourselves, fragmenting everything we perceive. As once we truly look within, we will recognise that the Source is already within us and everything we create in our outward experience is entirely self-created.

You experience everything within yourself! Spirit is the true reality, the physical simply mirrors that which is in spirit" stated Nexus.

Zion thought for a few moments about this, he found it difficult to integrate the thought that everything he seemingly saw outside of himself was actually a projection of his own consciousness. He would definitely have to sleep on that concept to let it sink in.

~ Level 7 ~

Kasima & The Interdimensional Warriors of the Light

O ne week later…

Zion's experiences had begun to heighten in clarity and frequency. His normal everyday life as a 16-year-old boy was becoming increasingly strange and surreal and his dream states had topped the charts of mind-blowing experiences. Everywhere he walked he could see peoples' aura's; he could sense their fears and as much as he could, he would reprogram their negative thoughts and transform them into positive to release the shadow Orion entities. Things were getting real.

That night when he lay down in bed and started to sip at his special fruit smoothie, Zion felt anxious but excited. Each time he entered the dream state something so out of this world would greet him and he was always worried he wouldn't know what to do. But each time he would call on his guides and they would help him through anything. He told himself not to worry, he had so much support and no one would let him down. As he finished off the smoothie, he begun to feel sleepy and when his head hit the pillow he was out.

Zion emerged into a cloud of mist, he couldn't see much, all he knew was he was floating in the sky and he could only see water below him and ships in the water. After some time floating in the misty air, he was able to land on a bridge. He sensed something of magnificent size next to him but couldn't see it straight away. He looked down at his hands, they were enormous man hands, definitely not his hands. He felt absolutely massive like a giant, the bridge was miniscule compared to his magnificent size upon it. He was wearing gladiator gear waiting for a battle to take place.

As Zion looked around him, he saw mythical lions parading around the scene with adorned frills around their necks. He knew this was in another time, another dimension but he wasn't sure where, it felt like somewhere in England. But this countryside had a dimensional overlay and that was where he was vibrating. He sensed that he was there in this place as a worker or a type of warrior. He knew there was more to this scene than he could see, he looked deeper into the void to pick up more information.

Moments passed and he began to see outlines of ships in the sky, the pilots of the craft did not want to be seen. They were on a very important mission. The vessels were correspondingly massive in size, they were dark coloured and were shaped like stingrays, they were beaming light into the earth through the water. The water was illuminating as they beamed the high frequency energy light into the earth beneath. Healing the earth, cleaning up the negative energies.

Zion was the leader of a squad of middle earth giant warriors of the light, protecting a group of extra-terrestrials healing and sending light to planet earth. He felt ancient, around a thousand years old, but he couldn't be certain. He had been waiting a long time to do this, waiting until the time was right. To protect and bring light to the surface, raising the vibration so healing could take place from all the trauma, there had been so much trauma. He had been holding the light for a very long time.

Far in the distance Zion saw an image of an enormous magnificent white mythical dragon appear in the sky flying towards him. It's white scales glistened in the light and it's long, pointed tail swung like a rudder manoeuvring the glorious beast. The dragons wings flapped with power and grace until it landed benevolently in front of Zion's giant warrior frame. She was absolutely stunning and held a calm energy of power and protection.

Zion knew this dragon, she was his protector in this life, she was always around, her name was Kasima. Around his neck he wore a white feather from one of her wings. Whenever he needed to connect with her, he would just touch the feather and call for her. The message she always relayed to him was to just trust, to trust in the unknown.

Kasima walked towards him with honour and poise, she leant down and motioned for Zion the warrior to jump on her back. Zion hoisted his enormous frame onto her silky white scales and held on for dear life. Even though Zion was gigantic he fit perfectly on top of Kasima's back.

She exploded upwards with immense power and control and began to head towards the stingray ships in the sky. Zion guessed they were going to investigate what was happening on board the craft. Kasima whirled and dove around the craft inspecting each one, trying to find the commander of the fleet. Finally, she found him, slowed down and swooped underneath the entrance of the ship. The door began to open and Zion was teleported inside the commander's ship. He wasn't sure what he was going to find but he heard Kasima say in his mind, trust in the unknown, which always calmed him down.

Zion was ushered by tall grey beings to the control centre of the ship where the commander sat awaiting his arrival.

"Hello Zion, my name is Commander Roth, I have been looking forward to meeting with you. You have been doing great work. We have come to assist you in your mission of raising the vibrational frequency of the planet earth. Our craft are specifically designed to infuse healing light energy into the deep grids of mother earth, we are activating them now. We siphon the negative residue away from the core and send it out to the Source to be renewed and recycled into positive energy. We call it transmutation; this is essentially what you are doing within your own body when you flip people's shadows and turn them to the light. You are accomplishing a massive feat Zion and we commend you for your tremendous efforts."

"Where are you from Commander?" asked Zion.

"I come from the Galactic Confederation, the council of nine, which is what you would call the ninth dimension. This avatar you see in front of you is not truly me, it is a physical version of what I am projecting from the higher realms for your comfort. This overlay you see with the giant warrior squad; the animal warriors and these ships is all just a hyperspace hologram shown to you so you can understand the help you are receiving. We support you completely in your mission and this is a representation of the kind of help you have on your side. We will not let you fail Zion. You must know that everything that is going to happen has already happened and you are just reviewing it in your mind. Time is an illusion and everything is in the now." stated the Commander".

Zion thought for a moment, deciding that this made him feel a lot better. The fact that he was not alone and he had the help of the giants and the confederation gave him confidence to continue on with more strength than he ever knew he had.

"Thank you, Commander, I appreciate the support. Is there anything I can do to better serve my mission?" asked Zion.

"Keep integrating the lessons each experience teaches you Zion, in time you will have integrated each and every fragment of existence back to yourself and then and only then will you be reunited as one with Source. This is the main event; this is what we are striving for" the Commander explained.

"Soon Zion, when the planetary sphere has reached a vibratory rate of critical mass the walk-ins will begin to descend", the Commander continued.

"What are walk-ins?" asked Zion.

"Do you remember the NPC's, the non-player characters you see walking about you, acting out plays around you creating catalysts for you to expand and eventually cause awakened thoughts in your mind? asked the Commander.

Zion nodded, agreeing with the Commander.

"Well Zion, those un-souled avatars will soon be incarnated by beings of the light, of a very high frequency. These enlightened high dimensional beings are coming from all over the galactic universe to help Gaia heal. The Earth will continue to be infused with more and more higher frequency ray light beams. This is so it can evolve high enough to house these high vibrational souls which has never happened in all of eternity. This is the main event we have all been waiting for, the emergence of the new Earth.

You must be vigilant in the maintenance of your physical avatar, the presence of these light beams and walk-ins can be unsettling to the unconditioned physical human body. They were not designed to hold such powerful frequencies and if they are not conditioned highly enough they will be destroyed.

I cannot tell you when this will happen. This upcoming event has no time stamp upon it as you know, it will only progress once the critical mass of positively orientated energy has been reached. The aid of these walk-in beings will be of great service to humanity and your mission, they will help you immensely. Just be strong Zion and know that help is on the way, it may come when you least expect it, but you will always be supported in the highest degree by the Galactic Confederation throughout all of the known Universe" said the Commander.

Zion wasn't completely sure what this all meant but he knew in time he would understand. He was having the time of his life; his life had never possessed so much meaning. He was excited to wake up in the morning and he was even more excited to go to sleep at night. His life had evolved into a metaphysical adventure and he had no idea where it would lead. He couldn't wait for the next moment that would arise and what he would experience and learn.

Zion walked to the window of the sting ray craft and looked out the window. Below, he could still see the giant warriors protecting the land and at this vantage point amongst the other ships he could see the healing light more clearly. It included all the colours of the rainbow and more, colours he had never seen before and could not name. The colours sparkled with a golden hue and he could feel the energy emanating from them all. It was the most powerful light imaginable, it was coming directly from Source, filtering through the holographic craft and into Mother Earth. Zion could almost feel the earth breathing a sigh of relief, renewing and beginning to pulsate with a higher frequency. It was working. He and his helpers were serving the planet. Zion felt accomplished, his work here tonight was complete, of course it continued without his awareness but for now he could relax.

He let out a sigh of relief and at once the giant warrior of light suit just fell to the ground and a light shot off to the heavens.

Zion awoke feeling completely rested and renewed. He had decided today he must talk to Zia and find out what had been going on with her and see if his experiences where somehow connected to hers. It was the weekend so he knew Zia would be in her room reading or on her laptop. He knocked on her door and she called for him to enter.

"Hey sis, how's it going?" asked Zion from the doorway.

"Yeah ok, what's up?" Zia responded.

"I just wanted to talk to you about our conversation the other week we had about your dreams. What's been happening?" Zion asked cautiously.

Zia was a very private person and wasn't the biggest conversationalist. She kept most things close to her chest. Zion didn't want to cross a line and get no information, but he had to know what had been going on.

"Oh, you know just weird dreams, that's all" said Zia.

Zion confided, "Yeah, I do know, I've been having them too."

"Really, what's been happening?" asked Zia.

Zion went into a big spiel about everything that had happened from the beginning when he met Nexus, to the Spiritual library, to his off-world experiences and the giant warriors. Zia sat in awe while he explained everything in precise detail, leaving nothing out. He had been dying to tell someone what had been happening but didn't know who he could trust to not think he had gone completely mad. Finally, he finished his entire story and complete silence fell on the room. Moments passed and Zia looked like she was in a trance but then suddenly she shook her head and spoke.

"Wow Zion, now I understand." She said.

"Understand what?" Zion asked.

"I have been having very similar experiences but with different circumstances. I met Nexus and I also went to the spiritual library and sat in the white chair in the experience room. I have also been on a mission to bring light to Mother Earth but in a more feminine way through healing souls" Zia stated.

"What do you mean, healing souls?" asked Zion.

"I work in the Motherboard etheric healing realm, where we heal souls. Any soul can come and be healed, all they need to do is ask. We work with incarnate souls still experiencing a life who are unwell and need to be patched up. We also work with souls that have passed on and are transitioning to their next incarnation. We help them heal their trauma and nourish them with sound and light to strengthen their vital energy. I work in the Motherboard department where I scan living humans for leaks" replied Zia.

Zion couldn't believe it; Zia had been having a mind-blowing experience all this time too and they had not yet seen each other in the dream state.

"Wow, how have we not seen each other in the dream state, or known that we have both been experiencing this strange phenomenon?" asked Zion.

"I don't know?" replied Zia.

Then a voice boomed over Zions thoughts. "You must only ask to meet, if this is your intention."

"Did you hear that?" Zion asked Zia.

"Yes" she replied. "Nexus!"

"I have an idea, tonight before we go to sleep, we must both hold the intention of meeting within the dream state. We need to see why this is happening to both of us. Deal?" asked Zion.

"Deal" said Zia.

Zion left Zia's room completely blown away by what they had discovered. He couldn't wait until night fell and they would unlock the mystery.

~ Level 8 ~

Vega & The Healing Realm

That night Zion lay crystalising his intention for the journey ahead. He intended to meet his twin sister within the dream state and understand their mission together, there must be a reason why they were both experiencing these off-planet phenomena. Once he felt he had crystalised his intention sufficiently he finished his smoothie and off he drifted.

Through the void he floated and drifted, through eternity and beyond, he had no sense of up or down and eventually the movement slowed and stopped and he found himself in a bright room filled with computers. These computers were highly advanced and technical, something from the future Zion thought.

Then along came a light being. He could just make out some of its facial features, it's eye's looked familiar.

"Zion, it's me Zia," the being whispered.

Zion stood shocked, Zia emanated a magnificent amount of pure golden light, he couldn't believe his eyes. His sister really was helping the higher realms, but what was this room for, he wondered.

"It is for healing of the DNA structure Zion, step over here and I will scan you. This scan will show any leaks you have in your field" Zia stated.

"Leaks, what do you mean leaks?" asked Zion, feeling a little worried.

"Throughout our human lives we can become defected, we can get sick or somebody may hurt us, which creates a kind of leak in our circuits, in the coding. It stops us from operating on all circuits available and diminishes our life force, our output power" explained Zia.

"How do you fix it?" asked Zion.

"Through sound and light Zion, we tune the circuits, and the whole template. The sound and light create a frequency vacuum effect and seals the leaks, it repairs any distortions within the human body at the level of the DNA. Your DNA is connected to the Motherboard where all instruction, the program of how to build the body, comes from. This entire place is the Motherboard command centre where we organise the whole of the DNA sequence and repair any faults that arise. There are multiple departments, each one specialising in a different area of expertise. I work here in the scanning centre, where I determine what distortions are in the DNA. I can then send the person onto the correct department to be healed if it is appropriate. Sometimes healing is not possible, we are not able to intervene in some cases. For example, if the person needs the distortion to learn an important lesson in their lifetime the distortion is paramount in their success even if it causes them discomfort and pain. Through discomfort and pain, we are forced to do things we would never have thought imaginable. This type of catalyst in our lives evolves and shapes us into different frequencies we would have never experienced. This is one of the important aspects of human life on planet earth, to experience all of the ups and downs that correspond to our emotional states. In other dimensions there is no such thing as pain, suffering or emotions, everything is perfect. In theory this sounds wonderful but excelled evolution can only come through heightened emotional response. Therefore, the planet Earth is the elite university of evolutional excellence, so much can be achieved in a relatively short space of time. Beings are lining up to come to Earth, there is not enough bodies to embody all that want to come" explained Zia.

"Wow, that's amazing, are we able to do this patching of the leaks for ourselves? asked Zion.

"Yes Zion, when you know the technique, you can do it yourself. You are the program and the programmer. You are the programmer of the code; the DNA activation is your software upgrade. I will teach you about the blueprint so you can become a master alchemy creator" said Zia.

Zia started explaining in great detail how to consciously manifest a timeline in the quantum field. She explained how through thought you create a certain frequency which creates a particle which then expands and projects itself as a blueprint into the hologram around you through the quantum field. Emotions are also measurements of frequency and become sonic imprints, a form of vibrational geometry. By combining an emotion (frequency/geometry) and a thought (blueprint) they collapse into one and become a geometric pattern hologram. Ultimately to manifest this holographic blueprint into a life structure is the goal of master creator.

Once you can hold your holographic imprint in your mind and project the visualisation into the quantum field it will begin to pulsate. With continued projection and focus on the emotion of this holographic imprint it will begin to become more potent, more vibratory and will vibrate at higher speeds. This is the beginning of it expanding into matter. You must continue to hold the highest frequency to express this high potency for expansion. The most potent emotion is love and by holding that potent emotion until a physical catharsis you may then let it go. Now you have the blueprint, the frequency now exists in the field, now you must take action and be relentless to crystalise it into matter. You will be shifting into a whole new timeline reality hologram, where your human body will be completely perfect with no leaks.

She also explained how the emotion of gratitude is the neutralising zero point. When you hold the emotion of gratitude, you can clear a hurtful event in your past for example just like shutting down a computer program you don't want to run anymore. This can reduce the severity and incidence of the leaks becoming a reality in your timeline.

Zion felt this information seemed similar to what Fior had explained to him on the blue planet about how the nimeo's worked. They too formed geographic patterns and manifested into matter.

"Magnificent, I will work on that. Do I have any leaks?" asked Zion.

"You do have some mild cracks; they have not quite formed into leaks yet but will eventually if we don't fix them now" stated Zia.

Zia showed Zion on the huge transparent computer screen in front of him a visual representation of himself reflected as an aura figure with an outline of sharp lines emanating from it. A deep red, blue outline was the closest to the body followed by a thick sky-blue layer. Then a deeper blue hue surrounded the sky-blue energy flowing into a fiery red out to the edges. In some spaces the thickness wasn't as dense as the rest of the areas. Mainly around Zion's torso, near his heart he assumed were the cracks Zia was referring to.

"We can fix this," Zia exclaimed excitedly. "Let's go see Vega, she will help you."

Zion followed Zia out the door and down a long corridor to a door on the right marked "Blueprint Manifesting". Before they could even think about knocking, a voice inside ushered them in. Zia opened the door and Zion peered through the opening, wondering what he was going to see. Once he stepped through the doorway, Zion was greeted with a magnificent outdoor garden landscape, an extremely colourful temple lay ahead of him. Zia took Zion inside the temple. High upon the ceiling, shining through windows surrounding the upper part of the temple, shone light through every gemstone you could imagine. There were blues, reds, greens, yellows, oranges, turquoise, every colour you could think of. The colours cast beautiful rays of light down onto the temple floor where the largest quartz crystal Zion had ever seen was fixed in the centre of the floor. Above the crystal, approximately three feet in the air, was a crystal platform hovering with nothing seemingly holding it up.

Vega stood up from her seated position on the floor. She too was a light being but she seemed different to Zia's appearance. She looked like she was from off planet, not of Earth. Which made sense as, this place was definitely not planet Earth. She glowed with a red hue which reminded Zion of Bobby's Dad, Alfred, he also glowed red but not quite as bright as Vega.

Vega began to speak "Yes Zion, red is the colour of healing directly specific to human healing. We use the vibratory frequency that red gives to heal cracks that are forming to heal instantly. You have some cracks around your heart, we will heal them now. If you would like to come and lay down, we can begin."

Zion walked towards Vega and she motioned for him to lay down near the quartz crystal. He lay down on a soft red velvet mattress and could immediately feel the floor vibrating beneath him. He then heard the soft sounds of a beautiful harmony playing in the background. It all felt very relaxing. Zion closed his eyes for a moment and when he opened them again, he was on the crystal platform in the middle of the temple hovering above the majestic quartz crystal. He was now in the centre of the room directly beneath where the colourful rays were converging. The light from above was filtering through him to the crystal below causing him to feel heightened vibrational frequencies.

"This, Zion, is the temple where people come to heal," started Vega. "Relax and let the light and the sound wash over you and be at one with you. The light will swirl around you and create a holographic imprint overlay and rejuvenate you to perfect health. Feel the waves of light colour energy take any distortions from your body, let it cleanse any negative energy from your soul. Feel the sense of peace that comes. Feel the loving energy through your whole body, every cell of your body. Let it tap into your heart space and strengthen your connection with Source. This is where your power is, this is where the magic is held. You must never forget, Zion, to always express with the emotion of love, it is the only way. Even in the darkest of times."

Zion came to after what felt like hours. He was back on the floor, on the red velvet mattress. Vega was looking into his eyes, checking that all the necessary work had been done to completion, that he was fully healed.

"How do you feel Zion?" asked Vega.

Zion sat up and looked around him. He felt amazing. More whole somehow. He thanked Vega and left the temple.

When he found Zia again, she explained that an emergency meeting had been called and they must hurry to attend. They entered an enormous round stadium where beings of light, and beings from off-planet all mingled around excitedly. Zia and Zion sat near the edge of the right wing anticipating something big. What looked like the head being emerged in the centre and began to welcome everyone.

"Good day all," she began. "As you all know our mission to heal and bring light to the Universe has been underway for eons. Our focus has been on planet Earth of late as it has been the most threatened by the negative forces. Due to our continued powerful efforts, we have caused a massive reduction of negative shadow energy and light is once returning to planet Earth. Although this is to be commended, it means the negative forces are even more determined to overthrow us. They have hacked into our mainframe and shut down some of our departments. These shutdown's have been initiated by the Orion group to disable our efforts as a fail-safe to guard against losing their hold on humanity. We must continue our resolve and stay committed to our intentions for the future of the Universe. Work will be done to protect the Motherboard and restore full operation to the mainframe. You all must continue your important work and remain in the highest frequency. We will take a moment to send love and light to our negative counterparts for the contrast they show us. We send gratitude to them for showing us the way of the light."

The whole of the stadium fell into a trance like state and each and every being began to hum a specific tone. Zion joined in and could feel the gratitude and love throughout the immense space. After a minute or so everyone left quietly to return back to their appropriate areas.

Zion turned to Zia and asked, "How does that work, sending love, light and gratitude to the negative entities? It's just so backwards to how humans react in our society throughout time."

"That's the point Zion exactly," Zia replied. "Humans have had it all wrong all these hundreds of years. By sending negative energy back to a negative energy experience it just multiplies the negative energy, compiling it on top of one another and increasing its strength. Like making a dark room darker by blocking out all of the light. But by sending positive high vibrational energy towards a negative energy, it lightens the load. Like turning on a light or opening a curtain, light casts out the darkness, transmuting negative to positive.

Forgiveness comes into play too because when you hold onto a negative emotion you funnel your energy continuously into that timeline, keeping it active. If you can forgive that emotion, experience, or person, they no longer have a hold over you, and you are no longer feeding it with your energy keeping it open. Remember also, gratitude is the zero point where you can refresh your timeline. So, gratitude even to a negative force can clear the bond you hold and cut ties with it."

"Wow Zia, you're absolutely right, I have learned all of those aspects but when you explain it all together like that it really makes a lot of sense. So, what can we do to help now? asked Zion.

"Just do what everyone has taught you Zion, you know everything within yourself" replied Zia. "Just tap into that and continue on your journey. They say that if everyone on the planet Earth just for one day could hold only positive thoughts, the Orion group would be cast from planet Earth for good. They would not be able to continue to resonate at the higher frequencies and would be forced to leave".

Zion awoke, amazed at how all of this information was finally sinking in. Now he knew what Zia's mission was, he felt more determined than ever. He had so much support surrounding him. It was becoming epic now, the Orion entities were fighting harder than they ever had and they had to be stopped.

~ Level 9 ~

Drago & The Underworld

Zion awoke in a dark cold musty space; he had no idea where he was but it felt ominous. He could hear loud sounds banging and clanging, and moans from miles away. Zion could hear the deep hum of machine running near him. He felt like he might be underground somewhere as the air felt thick and suffocating. He immediately remembered what all his guides had been telling him, "Remember to tap into your heart space and hold a high frequency, especially in the darkest situations." He knew what he had to do. He closed his eyes and focussed on the emotion of love. Once he held the frequency, he expanded it into his field. Light began to fill the space he lay in and images began to become clearer.

He was in an underground bunker. A large fan whirled around and around on one side of the wall, a type of ventilation system he figured. Zion looked down at his body and was somewhat surprised by what he saw. His skin was leathery and scaly and white in colour, and his body looked similar to a reptile. Was this the reptilian humanoid species that the Orion group hybridised to intermingle into the human population and better infiltrate our consciousness? Zion continued to hold his high frequency even though only a few months ago this situation would have scared the living crap out of him. But now he knew what he needed to do; all of his hard work had been to cast out these beings. He had an opportunity to find out how they thought, how they worked and what their major plan was. He could play along amongst them and infiltrate their demise from within.

Zion got up and walked to the door, bracing himself for whatever was going to happen outside of it. He swung the door open and walked into the large underground rock tunnel beginning to his right. He could hear grunts and groans and weird clicking and hissing sounds coming from that direction so he knew something was ahead.

Before long Zion came upon a large group of reptilian beings having some sort of meeting within a large cavern. He slid behind a nearby wall to watch from afar. Some of the beings stood towering at twelve to thirteen feet tall. They had white skin like he did and seemed to be the top leaders as they were gathered in the centre of the space higher than all the others. There were also a group of them that were sable black which seemed to be another highly ranking group to their right. The rest of the creatures mingled a level down and looked to be a mix of red, tan and green with varying heights and features. The creatures seemed to be devising a plan of action but Zion couldn't understand what they were saying. But then he realised if he was in this body, he could understand if he could just tune into the frequency without letting it take over his emotions.

With concentration, Zion was able to understand their language, it was very course, but he got the idea. They were speaking about their survival; they were worried that over the past few months their source of food was dwindling. Intuitively Zion picked up something from Nexus as he was wondering what they fed on.

"They feed on negative energy Zion, all of the fear, depression, sadness, anger and hatred you have been transmuting from the people of earth's shadows. They call it 'loosh' and they are utterly dependent on this energy for their survival, they cannot go on without it," stated Nexus.

Zion came to learn that the reptilian race called themselves 'The Drago' and had formed an allegiance with the influential leaders of planet Earth. They had manipulated these human leaders to do their work for them, to bring society under the grips of fear and darkness. A small group of these humanoid leaders stood segregated from the rest of the Drago with somewhat worried looks on their faces. They were the ones who had caused the shadow within and were doing the work for the Drago, generating the loosh for them, feeding them. These leaders had been keeping the society of Earth in fear and panic just enough to siphon the dark energy to feed their Draconian superiors.

Zion began to receive downloads directly correlated to the body he was in; he now knew where he was. They were situated below the surface of Antarctica near an ancient portal that was the only one left in the whole of planet Earth still in working order. The Orion group had been able to pierce the veil of protection at a specific time of darkness, when their hold had been the strongest and they were overriding planet Earth. They seeded this hybridised species of reptilians close to the portal underground in the hope that they would go undetected. They had accomplished this for many years, and only now had someone realised what they were doing. They had been discovered but they didn't know it yet.

Out of nowhere, a sable black Drago touched Zion on the shoulder and motioned for him to join the meeting. He couldn't blow his cover, so with all his confidence he walked on up to the massive group of Draconian and the small group of humans and took his place amidst the white skinned group. They all hissed with delight when they saw Zion, and he sensed he held a high standing amongst these beings. They trusted him and looked to him for guidance. Zion needed some time to think about his next move but sitting in the company of them all was very unnerving, and his thoughts kept darkening.

Zion continued to tap into his heart space and hold strong, but it was an enormous challenge. One of the white Drago's was the one doing most of the talking. He spoke of the diminishment of their loosh and that it was all to do with the Galactic Confederation increasing their efforts of bringing light to the planet. They knew more and more light beings where siphoning light energy into planet Earth and they knew more and more people were transmuting their shadows.

Without warning the speaker turned to Zion and asked, "What do you think, Thysais?"

Zion gulped and looked around; they were all staring at him with anticipation. Waiting for him to say something profound. Zion thought for a moment, he had to find out if what Zia had said was correct.

He began speaking with confidence. "What do we all agree is our biggest threat, what would unequivocally bring us down without fail, who can tell me?" Zion posed as a question to the audience.

One of the red Drago called from the sides, "Peace on Earth!" He exclaimed. "If all of the humans held positive thoughts for an extended time, we would have nothing to feed from. We would be forced to leave and would never be able to return."

"Yes!" Zion shouted, knowing this answered his question perfectly. "Well then, we must stop this from happening at all costs" he exclaimed, to keep up appearances.

Zion thought for a moment, devising a plan of action, something that could stop the wrath of the Drago, or at least slow them down. Then an idea came to him, it was perfect, it was magnificent, if he could conger up all the power that the plan needed.

He stood amongst the demonic creatures, their darkness filling every space around him, their dark demeanour trying to infest his pure vibration, but Zion stood strong. First, he tapped into his heart space, the space where Treeadoor taught him all his power came from, the space where he could manifest the highest of frequencies. He closed his eyes trying to block out the surrounding distractions. His body jolted from the increase in amplification. The reptilian avatar he embodied began to shake and vibrate and within seconds it simply fell to the floor revealing the human Zion within. Zion stood exposed with a look of shock on his face, he didn't expect to face this battle in his own skin but if that is what was required then bring it on, he thought.

One by one the Drago started to recognise that something unusual was happening. They saw the remains of their pure white Dragonian master lying on the floor beside Zion and began to piece the narrative together. They began to lunge at him, ripping shreds from his clothing as he ran for cover. While Zion ran, he focussed on keeping his frequency as high as possible, not letting the negative energy enter even his thoughts. He remembered how Zia had taught him about shifting timelines and how the emotion of gratitude can neutralise and over-ride a negative timeline. He focussed on the emotion of gratitude, building the potency as magnificently as he could.

Suddenly, a vision of eyes came into view within his mind's eye. The eyes were of a dragon, a white dragon, Kasima had come to help him. Within moments, his body as Zion had morphed into the body of the dragon Kasima and he was flying high above the beasts. As he got higher and higher, he was able to look down upon the creatures below him, they were snarling and biting, looking at him with the intent of death on their reptilian faces. Zion held his energy, and he began to expand it, he extended it out from his body first, then with each deep breath he multiplied and increased it further and further outwards.

Zion remembered Zia's words, "To master the alchemy of creation, you must feel it, project it, and believe it. This will then expand the energy in order to shift your creation into reality. Then you become the creator of your destiny. Zion felt the emotions, he projected them out into the field, he held a strong belief in the manifestation process and when he felt it crystalise he released it.

Suddenly, flashes of white light began exploding outwards from his body, pulsating like toroidal waves emanating from his heart centre. All Zion could see around him was bright white light that glistened with golden particles. The Drago were dropping like flies, their dense physical bodies could not hold the intensity of Zion's light. They began to join their white leader, laying lifeless on the floor of the dark dingy underground dungeon. He looked over to where the humans were standing only moments earlier and saw that they too had succumbed to the powerful light.

When Zion felt he had emanated enough light he began to slow his breathing and float down to the surface of the demonic underworld. He looked around him in horror, knowing that the demise of these creatures was inevitable, but looking at them now brought a sadness to Zion that he didn't expect. He sat surrounded by lifeless bodies for what seemed like eternity with his dragon head lowered to the ground.

"Well done, Zion!" He heard Nexus say in his mind. "Do not feel regret, it was time for these entities to leave this planet. This was meant to be, all is well. All disabled grids are now active."

"Thanks Nexus" Said Zion "I want to go home now."

"Yes Zion, you may leave now your job here is done."

Zion took a deep breath and within moments entered back into his daytime realm, in his bed, glad to be in one piece.

~ Level 10 ~

Eli & The Holding Cell

When Zion awoke the next day, he still felt uneasy about what had happened during his dream state mission. He had never killed anyone in his life or ever even wanted to, he just put into effect everything he had learned over the past few months. But, he guessed, this was what it was all leading up to, the Orion group needed to be stopped and cast out of planet Earth. He presumed he hadn't actually killed them; they had just left their physical avatars and departed the realm of Earth. Nexus had commended him on his efforts, but he still felt a twang of remorse. Zion wondered if this meant his mission was over, he had defeated the Drago, what else was there to do?

The rest of the day continued on the same way, he felt uneasy and unsure of what he should do. He decided he needed to talk to a familiar friend, really talk it out, verbalise it and see if that shifted any of his remorseful emotions about the entire situation.

Zion decided to visit his best friend Eli, they hadn't hung out in ages as Zion had been so preoccupied with everything going on in his strange new world. He wanted to explain to Eli what had been happening, so he knew he still wanted to be best friends.

As Zion walked into Eli's bedroom, he knew immediately something was wrong, there was a dark cloud surrounding Eli and he looked really down.

"What's up Eli, sorry I haven't been hanging out lately, life has been hectic!" said Zion. "I've got a massive story to tell you," he continued.

"Hey dude," replied Eli, "I'm ok just feeling a bit low that's all. Come in."

Zion knew what he had to do but first he wanted to explain some of the events that had been occuring so Eli could better understand his mission. He began to tell Eli everything right from the beginning, with every detail imaginable. Eli just sat stunned like he was stuck to his bed, eyes gazing wide and mouth partly open. Every now and then he would nod or ask "How" or "Why" to what Zion was telling him. Zion felt relieved to tell his best friend what had been going on, he hadn't meant to keep it secret, it had all been pretty overwhelming.

Once Zion finished his story Eli had lots of questions and they spoke well into the evening. Zion left Eli's house feeling happy and felt he had cheered Eli up too; well he hoped so anyway.

That night, when Zion drifted off into his dream state, he had forgotten to cast his protection shield. When he awoke in the dream, he found himself in a form of burning hell. Zion was trapped in a small cell, the size of an animal cage, and around him all he could see was fire and smoke. Caverns of burning coals, were strewn as far as his could see through the thick black intoxicating smoke. There was hardly any light to see in the depths of this ominous landscape. Zion's breath became quick and panicked, he had never seen such a frightening scene. He had no idea why he was in such a harsh environment. Then he realised, maybe it had to do with what had happened last night. Maybe the Drago were able to drag him into their new world where they could torture him for the rest of his life. All he had learnt was wiped from his conscious memory, he forgot to tap into his heart space, he forgot to keep his frequency high even in the darkest of times as he had been taught time and time again.

But then, Zion looked down at his hands, they looked familiar and similar to his own but they weren't his hands. He continued to look at the rest of his body to understand who he was this time. He couldn't believe it; he was wearing the same t-shirt Eli was wearing the evening before when they were hanging out. Wait a minute, was he Eli?

A strong "Yes" boomed in his mind. Ok, this was weird, he had never been one of his friends before. But more importantly, where the hell was he, he thought. He needed some help with this situation and decided to call out to Nexus for some insight.

"You called, Zion" he heard Nexus ask in his mind.

"Yes, thanks Nexus, where am I and why am I here?" Zion asked, still feeling intimidated by his surroundings.

"Before I explain Zion I need you to calm down," said Nexus calmly. "Evoke your white light pyramid of protection, remember to tap into your heart space, raise your frequency, and recollect this is all just an illusion. Nothing can harm you".

"Yes, thanks Nexus, it was just so overwhelming for a moment there, I lost my mind," replied Zion, a little embarrassed.

"You must make these fundamental rules your ingrained instincts, Zion. In every situation you must not even think about your reaction, it should just happen like a program automatically," stated Nexus. "We must imbed these programs into your main frame, I will begin the download, it may take some time. In the meantime we must deal with the mission at hand".

"You are in a form of Hell; well a representation of what Eli believes is Hell anyway. What you must understand by now Zion, is that our thoughts and our beliefs create our reality."

Zion agreed.

"Well Zion, Eli has been taught his whole life by his mother that he must be good and just and become a perfect person and if he doesn't, he will be dammed to Hell for all eternity. When you went to see him today his shadow was growing, he had been feeding it with thoughts of not being good enough.

What you don't know is that last night when you set off your sonic boom of golden white light and cast the negative Drago entities off Earth, the ones that were in that very moment syphoning shadow energy from the humans, became passengers. This indicates a fragment of their darkest essence is now attached to the human they were draining off. Their physical bodies were discarded, and their etheric bodies have moved from this realm but a small fragment of their dark soul is stuck here until the humans they are attached to release them.

When you told Eli your story, he connected with it but also felt confused, as what you were telling him is possible was never possible in his reality. His belief system is different to yours. His ingrained belief program of not being good enough and in turn being damned to hell had manifested into a pocket reality" stated Nexus.

Zion thought for a moment, 'what was a pocket reality and how could he break himself free from it?'.

"A pocket reality Zion, is a new timeline platform possibility someone has created in their mind through a strong belief in something. Their belief is so strong that they don't even question it, it is their truth. Eli's truth was that he was going to be sent to eternal hell. The attachment of the Drago has now heightened this dark shadow influence on him and sent him deeper than he has even gone before. So now you find yourself in his internal reality, his internal Hell, a holding cell of sorts where neither of you can progress in your evolution until you can break him free and in turn release yourself. You are held behind a fire wall of sorts where virtually no one can assist you. You need to work this one out for yourself as we cannot break through the fire wall" declared Nexus.

Zion felt a pang of nerves shoot through his stomach, but he knew he was prepared for this; he wouldn't have been put in the situation if he wasn't ready. You are only given what you are ready to handle his guides had taught him. He just had to focus on the mission at hand and do all he could to break himself and his best friend free from the grips of the energy sucking vampires, the Drago.

While he sat in his holding cell devising a plan, he noticed the flames became taller, hotter, and more ferocious. Zion began to tap into his heart space visualising Treeadoor and the strong connection they had. He began remembering all of the experiences he had had over the past few months. All the new and fascinating friends he had met, including Custos his long-time friend from the spiritual library. Fior, his multidimensional colleague on the blue planet that had taught him all about hydro-energy. Then he remembered the warriors of the light and Kasima the dragon who was his protective spirit animal and was with him eternally. He began to feel so supported and loved. Then Vega the healing light being, and of course his twin sister Zia, who now knew everything and joined him in the adventure of a lifetime.

Suddenly a feeling of hot lava took over Zion, it came running down the hot wasteland into his cell. He couldn't move away from it, and it began to encapsulate him. Zion held his vibratory rate strong; he visualised his protection shield but nothing could stop the scorching liquid. It filled the cell and melted over his entire body. Within moments it had merged and crystalised Zion's body within it. Zion couldn't move, he was trapped inside this molten rock, fused in a holding cell of beliefs. He couldn't tap into Nexus anymore; he couldn't contact anyone.

He was stuck in this fiery holding dimension, he thought, possibly for eternity.

The End...

About the Author

Natalie Watson, a beyond quantum healing practitioner and metaphysical researcher, was born and raised in the beautiful Fleurieu Peninsula Coast, south of Adelaide, in South Australia and lives with her long-time partner, son and menagerie of animals.

With a deep interest in the healing arts, Natalie pursued study in complimentary medicine to later realise that energy medicine and hypnosis was the key to healing mentally, physically and spiritually. Her continued research led her to become a beyond quantum healing practitioner where she enters clients into a hypnotic state and guides them in experiencing appropriate lives where they can find closure and healing in the etheric realms. Her clients experience many wonderful scenes of past, present or future lives to aid them on their continued evolution.

The fascination in this field led Natalie to many and varied metaphysical and scientific universal knowledge. It is through these uncovered concepts she felt the need to share some of her own, and her clients, experiences through hypnosis with the wider world. Natalie hopes to build her hypnosis career and begin specialising with people who have had unexplained and extra-terrestrial phenomena contact.

Even though she and her clients have absolute faith in the information that comes through in the hypnosis sessions. Natalie decided to convey her message through a fictional three-part series to make it accessible to everyone, especially younger adults.

She hopes that her epic fantasy adventure opens the minds of people and shows them what they are truly capable of and how powerful they truly are.

If you wish to contact Natalie about her work or her private beyond quantum healing sessions please send an email to bodytemple@live.com.au or visit her page at https://www.facebook.com/BodyTemple-Expansion-286934232140730

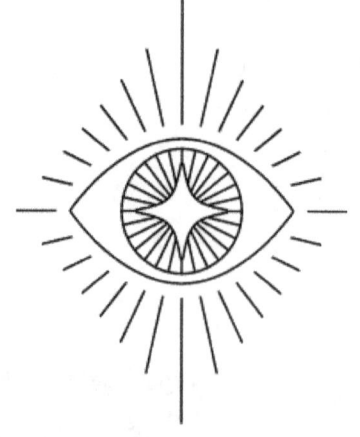

Body Temple Publishing